THE SECRET EXPLORERS
AND THE DESERT DISAPPEARANCE

CONTENTS

Chapter One
GLEEFUL GARDENING

Leah turned her face up to the sunshine pouring into her garden. It was a beautiful day in Oxford, with birds singing their hearts out and butterflies flittering around in little dabs of yellow, brown, and white.

She was installing her new watering kit for the garden. She had already laid the flexible pipe, with its carefully spaced watering holes, through all her raised beds, to make sure the water reached even the farthest patch of carrots and broccoli. It was cleverly designed to release a small amount of water per hour, so that the soil had a chance to absorb the moisture before it evaporated.

Now all she had to do was fix the pipe to the large rain barrel that caught the rainfall from the gutters on the house, and her new watering system was good to go.

Leah patted the rain barrel and listened to the dull echo that told her that it was full. *Kiki would love this*, she thought, thinking of her tech expert friend as she clipped the pipe into place and set the digital timer.

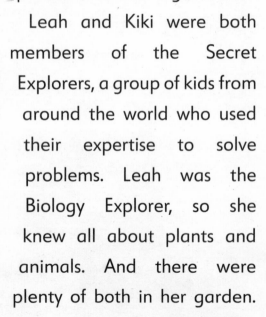

Leah and Kiki were both members of the Secret Explorers, a group of kids from around the world who used their expertise to solve problems. Leah was the Biology Explorer, so she knew all about plants and animals. And there were plenty of both in her garden.

Leah had planted lots of flowers for the bees, butterflies and insects among her vegetables: lavender and black-eyed susans, bright pink cosmos flowers, and heavy yellow dahlias. There weren't enough insects these days, so Leah did what she could to care for them. Today she was planting a calendula, a favorite with the bees. She grinned when a bee flew into the plant before she had even patted down the soil around its roots.

Leah suddenly caught sight of something on her garden shed door. It glimmered and flickered. *Is that a butterfly?* she wondered. She looked closer and grinned in delight as she realized it was actually the compass symbol of the Secret Explorers. It matched the badge she wore on her shirt. *We've got a new mission!*

Leah wiped her muddy hands on her jeans and pushed open the shed door. She squinted in the blinding light, and felt a cool wind blow over the top of her head. When she blinked to clear her eyes, she saw the familiar surroundings of Exploration Station: the HQ of the Secret Explorers.

The gleaming black stone walls were very different from the lush greenery of Leah's garden. Displays of objects collected by the Explorers sat in glass cases around the room. Computers that monitored the missions hummed and winked against one wall, while a group of comfy chairs and sofas stood together in the corner. On the polished floor was a huge map of the world, and the domed ceiling showed the infinite sprinkle of the Milky Way.

"Leah, here!" Leah called, making her way toward the sofas.

The door began to glow again. The other Explorers were arriving.

"Gustavo, here!" called the History expert.

"Connor, here!" The Marine Biology expert from the United States was next, wiping his wet feet on the mat.

A girl with short curly hair appeared next, blinking through her glasses. "Kiki, here!" she said. Kiki was from Ghana, and specialized in Computers and Technology.

"Ollie, here!" said the Rainforest Explorer, rubbing a hand through his messy blond hair with a yawn. "I think."

"Did we wake you up, Ollie?" said a girl with wide brown eyes and thick black hair. She laughed at the look on Ollie's face.

"Roshni, here!" Roshni was from India, and was the Explorers' Space expert.

"Cheng, here!" The Geology expert from China was next, his hands full of pebbles. It looked like he'd been beachcombing.

The last to arrive was a girl with a dinosaur slide in her hair. "Tamiko, here!" she said. Tamiko was from Japan, and she knew all about dinosaurs.

"So what do you think our mission will be?" said Gustavo eagerly.

"Going back to bed?" suggested Ollie with another yawn.

The map on the floor suddenly lit up. The Explorers hurried over.

"That's Mexico," said Connor. Mexico! The Explorers looked at each other eagerly. What was happening in Mexico?

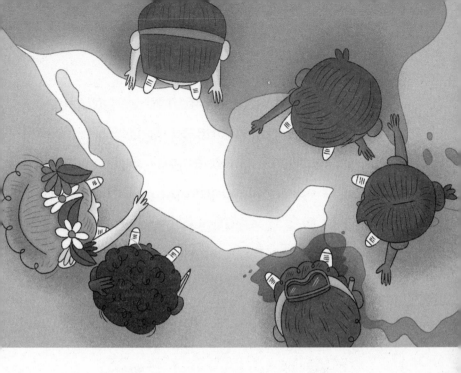

Next, a screen appeared. At first all Leah could see was swirling dust and some cacti. Then she spotted something with gray-brown fur, slinking across the sandy landscape.

"Wolves!" she said in delight. "Our mission must be to help the wolves!"

"You'll definitely be picked, Leah," said Kiki. "You're the animal expert, after all."

Leah really hoped so. She loved wolves!

And she had always wanted to visit Mexico. "Yes!" she cheered as the compass badge on her shirt lit up.

"Wait, what?" said Connor as his badge lit up too. "I would not put wolves and marine biology together."

"Maybe they're underwater wolves," Leah joked. "Looks like we're teammates, Connor." Picking the Marine Biology expert seemed like a strange choice, but the Exploration Station was never wrong!

Kiki headed for a large red button on the wall and pressed it firmly. There was a shudder and a groan as the floor opened. Up rose . . .

a battered old go-kart, with peeling paint and a dented steering wheel.

"Hey, Beagle," said Leah, giving the go-kart an affectionate pat.

The other Explorers took their places at the computers, ready to provide any help Leah or Connor might need on their mission. Leah and Connor sat in the battered metal seat of the Beagle.

"Ready?" Leah asked Connor.

"Bring on the underwater wolves," said Connor, punching the air.

"Good luck!" shouted the others as Leah put her hands on the steering wheel.

The Beagle began to shudder and groan. Leah clung tightly to the wheel and squinted in the bright light that suddenly surrounded her once more. Her hair blew around her head. A warm, sandy wind was hitting the go-kart, which was changing beneath Leah's hands. Everything was getting bigger. Leah felt a hat drop on to her head. Tight belt buckles snapped around her waist.

"Whoa!" shouted Connor as the light began to fade. He coughed in the dust that now surrounded them. "Sand on my tongue. Sand on my tongue!"

Leah flapped her hand in front of her face, coughing. The dust was thick, and she couldn't see a thing. Where were they?

Chapter Two
THE DUSTY DESERT

The sandy wind whirled around the Beagle. Not only was it dusty; it was hot as well. Connor was sitting beside Leah, buckled in as tightly as she was. There was a bright metal frame and a sturdy canvas roof over their heads, and the sides were open. The Beagle had four chunky wheels, and a solid metal chassis. It had transformed into a desert buggy!

"These should keep us cool," said Connor, looking at the loose cotton tops and trousers they were now wearing.

"This too!" Leah said, pointing at her hat. Connor was wearing a floppy, wide-brimmed hat that matched her own.

She leaned forward and wiped the dust off the dashboard. Now the bright lights of the Beagle's top-of-the-range navigation system blinked and shone.

"We are in Mexico, right?" Connor checked.

Leah nodded. "The Chihuahuan Desert in Mexico, to be exact," she said, tapping the dashboard to show Connor the map.

"Chihuahua, like the dog?" Connor asked.

"Chihuahuas came from Mexico originally," Leah explained.

The Beagle beeped in relief as the dust finally cleared. Leah gasped at the sight. She'd never seen a landscape like this before. The rocks and earth were a range of reds and yellows, grays and whites. She could see cacti on the dry desert floor, and the bright blue sky which stretched over their heads. Leah could see a bird of prey circling high above them in the hot desert air. By its call, she guessed it was a kite—a type of hawk.

There was a sudden flash of movement to the right of the buggy. Leah glimpsed something slinking away beyond a gnarled cactus—something with dappled, coppery fur and a short, black-tipped tail.

"A bobcat!" she exclaimed. "Look!"

"I'm kind of busy looking at the snake," said Connor, a little anxiously.

Leah twisted her head to see the curled shape of a snake, snoozing on a warm red rock close to the buggy. It had markings like a tabby cat and a distinctive lump on the end of its tail.

"Oh wow, a rattlesnake!" Leah gasped.

The snake woke up. Raising its head, it shook its tail at the Beagle as a warning. The dusty rattling sound sent a prickle of excitement and fear down Leah's back. It was a beautiful animal, but she was glad they were in the buggy. Oxford didn't have any wild rattlesnakes, that was for sure.

"This place is *incredible*," she breathed. She rested her hands on the Beagle's steering wheel and looked at Connor. "So what now? We have a mission to find."

"Let's start driving," suggested Connor. "Maybe away from the snake?"

There was a dusty track just ahead of them, winding away through the glimmering desert. Leah revved the Beagle's engine and they began to bump through the Chihuahuan desert. The horizon shimmered in the heat and the sun battered down. Leah was glad she was wearing a hat.

"There's a sign," said Connor suddenly. The sign was large and colorful, planted almost at the end of the track. It said CHIHUAHUA WILDLIFE REFUGE. Away in the distance, Leah glimpsed some slinking gray shapes among the rocks.

"Wolves," she said. She grinned at Connor. "This must be the place."

The track grew rockier and more uneven. Leah carefully guided the Beagle toward a

group of long, low huts with colorful shutters in the windows. A girl about their age appeared at the door, shading her eyes. She pushed up the sleeves of her sand-colored T-shirt and came to greet them.

"Hola," she said politely. "Hello! Can I help you?"

Leah introduced herself and Connor. "We're actually hoping we can help you," she said, a little shyly.

The girl broke into a wide smile. "That's wonderful!" she exclaimed. "You are very welcome. We need all the help we can get."

She told them her name was Rosa, and she worked at the refuge with her parents.

"So what do you do here?" Connor asked, looking around at the dusty landscape and scattered huts.

"We are helping the Chihuahuan Desert's Mexican wolf population," Rosa explained. "Numbers are dwindling. People used to hunt wolves, you see. Some people still do."

Leah made a face. She hated to think of the magnificent animals being hunted.

"We have fewer than two hundred wolves left in the wild," Rosa went on. "So we are working on a breeding program, to increase the numbers."

"And how's it going?" Connor asked.

Rosa beamed. "One of our wolves is pregnant," she said proudly. "We are all very excited!"

Leah grinned. Wolves were great, but wolf cubs were next-level great! She couldn't wait to get started on this mission!

"Would you like to see how we monitor

our wolves?" Rosa asked.

"Would we ever!" enthused Leah.

Rosa laughed. "Come with me," she said, and beckoned them into one of the huts.

The inside of the hut was a surprise. Among cool white walls and beneath humming ceiling fans, there were rows of computer monitors. Each monitor showed a different part of the wildlife sanctuary: rocks, hills, trees—and wolves, sleeping in the sun and playing in the dust.

"We try to keep an eye on them all," Rosa said, guiding Leah and Connor toward a monitor in the corner of the room. "But here is the monitor that we are most interested in right now."

Leah and Connor stared at the screen. It showed a small, empty cave set into a hillside.

"Is there supposed to be a wolf in there?" Connor asked.

Rosa frowned at the monitor. "This is where our pregnant wolf should be," she said in surprise.

Leah studied the monitor carefully.

There was absolutely no sign of life in the den.

"She was there earlier . . ." said Rosa. She suddenly looked very worried. "But now she is gone! This is bad news. We need to find her before she gives birth. Wolf cubs are so vulnerable when they are newborns." She looked helplessly at Leah and Connor. "We have to find her. It's vital that she gives birth where we can see her, so we can help her if she needs us. Her cubs are crucial for our breeding program!"

Leah and Connor exchanged a quick glance. Finally, they understood the mission. Find the mother wolf—and keep her safe!

Chapter Three
WHERE'S THE WOLF?

Out in the preserve, there was no track at all. Leah drove the Beagle through the rocks and cacti, clinging tightly to the steering wheel. Rosa sat in the back of the buggy, biting her nails anxiously.

"I'm sure we'll find her," Connor reassured Rosa. "How big is the preserve?"

"Around three hundred square miles," said Rosa.

Connor went a little pale. "That's . . . big," he said at last.

"She could be anywhere," Rosa said, with panic in her voice.

They drove on in silence. Leah gazed around at the sprawling rocks, spiky plants, and hills. This was going to be hard. Much harder than she had expected.

"Are you from a conservation center, too?" Rosa asked as they bumped along.

Connor glanced at Leah. "We're from an organization . . . that solves problems," he said carefully.

Rosa looked interested. "And is this place in Mexico?"

Connor was saved from answering by the sudden sound of barking. Leah slammed on the brakes. Racing toward them in a blur of yellow-brown fur were some young cubs.

"Are these wolf cubs?" said Connor as the youngsters leaped and prowled around the buggy, sniffing at the wheels.

"They're definitely cubs of some kind," said Leah, amused to see the young animals jumping around. "But maybe they're too small to be wolves?"

"You're right. They're not wolves," Rosa agreed. "They're young coyotes."

Now Leah could see that the little animals had pointed ears rather than the rounded ears of wolves. She laughed at the young coyotes as they prowled and tumbled around the wheels of the Beagle. One minute they were pouncing on the buggy itself, the next they were turning on each other in a whirl of playful fur and teeth.

Leah started up the engine again, very carefully. The coyotes leaped back in surprise, then chased the Beagle enthusiastically as the buggy picked up speed. Eventually they grew bored and fell away, racing back into the desert and barking at each other.

The Chihuahuan Desert was extraordinarily beautiful. Leah couldn't believe the number of different creatures they saw as the Beagle churned through the dust: birds, and reptiles, and more coyotes gathered in sociable groups in the sun.

"That's a Texas horned lizard," Rosa said, pointing at an alarming-looking scaly creature basking on a hot rock. She had to raise her voice as the Beagle was rattling over some especially bumpy ground. "They can shoot blood from the side of their eyes to scare off predators!"

Connor looked a little green.

Leah saw another rattlesnake. It wasn't sleeping this time, but moving in a strange, rippling way across the ground. Leah knew it was called 'sidewinding,' and was a common way for snakes to move across smooth surfaces. It also looked different from the snake she and Connor had seen earlier, with stronger, darker markings.

"Black-tailed rattlesnake," Rosa explained. "We have thirty-seven different species of rattlesnake in Mexico. In fact," she added proudly, "over ninety percent of the world's rattlesnakes live in my country."

"That's a lot of rattlesnakes," said Connor weakly. His eyes widened and he drew his legs a little more tightly inside the Beagle. "Oh, boy. Is that a tarantula?"

A huge, hairy spider was crouching in the shadow of a rock. Its furry blond legs cast menacing shadows on the ground.

"You aren't afraid are you, Connor?" Leah teased.

"I don't like spiders that big," Connor confessed.

Rosa laughed. "That's a desert tarantula. They are actually very gentle creatures that won't hurt people." She stopped laughing and sighed. "But if only we could see the wolf."

It was true. For all the creatures they had passed, they had yet to see a single wolf.

"How can so many different creatures live in the desert?" Connor asked. "It's so hot. And I haven't seen any water at all!"

"They adapt," Leah explained. "Over millions of years, these animals have developed ways of surviving in this harsh environment. Desert tarantulas dig burrows that shelter them from the heat. Lizards have very thick skin to stop the water inside their bodies from evaporating." She squinted in the sun. "We'll have to adapt to the desert, too," she added. "But at least we're already wearing the right clothes and hats to protect us. And we have food and water in the trunk, right Beagle?"

The desert buggy beeped in agreement, startling Rosa.

The landscape was growing hillier as the Beagle drove onward. Leah's eyes swept the endless horizon, hoping to see the familiar loping shape of a wolf. But there was nothing. Nothing wolf-shaped, anyway.

"Wow!" she exclaimed, suddenly slamming on the brakes. Connor and Rosa both looked startled. "A Lloyd's hedgehog cactus!"

"A Lloyd's what now?" asked Connor, cramming his hat back on his head.

Leah leaped out of the buggy and crouched down to study the neat, cone-shaped cactus with its pink and orange flowers. "A Lloyd's hedgehog cactus," she repeated in excitement.

"They are super rare. Look at these flowers! And these stripes!"

The sturdy little cactus was very pretty, with its candy-pink stripes, bright flowers and thick white spikes.

"I don't know how plants survive out here," said Connor, squinting up at the wide blue sky.

"Desert plants are very good at storing water inside their thick stems," Leah said, straightening up.

She suddenly stopped with a gasp and crouched down again. Gently, she pulled out a little clump of gray fur, which had been caught on the cactus's white prickles. The fur was thick and strong, with a distinctive earthy smell.

"Wolf fur!" Rosa exclaimed. She sprang out of the Beagle. "This could be our pregnant wolf! Is there any more? Can you see tracks, maybe?"

Connor hurriedly unbuckled his seatbelt and joined Leah and Rosa as they hunted around. Everyone was filled with excitement at the chance discovery of the fur. It was a sign, Leah felt sure. A sign that the wolf was nearby.

"Here!" Connor shouted after a few moments.

The dusty ground just beyond the little cactus had been scuffed up. Leah could see the prints of a large, doglike foot pad.

"Yes!" Rosa cried. "Wolf prints. Now we can follow them and find our wolf!"

Chapter Four
CHIHUAHUAN DESERT LIFE

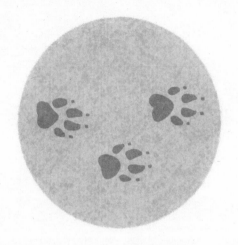

Leaving the Beagle parked beside the little pink flowering cactus, Connor, Leah, and Rosa started following the trail of wolf prints on foot. Away from the protection of the desert buggy's canvas roof, it wasn't long before Leah really began to feel the burn of the sun through the top of her hat.

Although she was hot, she didn't notice any sweat. The air here was so dry that it evaporated right away. It made a change from England—but Leah also knew that there was a danger of dehydrating. Humans aren't as good at storing water as cacti, she thought. She had made sure to take some bottled water from the Beagle's trunk.

The wolf prints wound steadily through the dust and rocks. Sometimes the marks were clear and easy to follow. Other times they were scuffed up, as if the wolf had decided to break into a trot.

Suddenly, the trail stopped. Rosa knelt down and studied the ground. Leah took off her hat and flapped the brim toward her face for a little breeze.

"I can't find any more tracks," Rosa said anxiously. "The ground here is too rocky and dry. What are we going to do now?"

To Leah's surprise, Connor gave a broad smile. "Don't worry," he said. "I've seen something that will help us."

"Where?" said Leah, looking around.

"Have you noticed how there are more plants growing around here?" Connor asked.

Leah had been so distracted by the cacti that she hadn't noticed the soft green fuzz of plants growing closer to the ground, or the prickly pear shrubs.

Something small and furry scurried past her feet. She heard the sound of birdsong, too.

"There are more animals as well," Leah said aloud.

"And we're heading downhill," said Connor triumphantly. "There must be water nearby! What if our wolf went in search of a drink?"

"Great idea!" Rosa exclaimed. "Let's find out!"

They hurried on. Leah heard more birdsong. Everything felt more lush, the farther down the hill they went. She was very glad to have the Marine Biology Explorer with her on this mission. Even in the desert, his knowledge was coming in useful.

Leah gasped as they went past one final dusty outcropping of rocks. A great lake stretched before them, blue and sparkling in the sun. Its banks were green with soft grass. Clusters of animals gathered around the

shore with their heads bent toward the water. A heavy splash startled Leah, and she saw a large bird rising from the water with a glittering fish in its talons.

"A lake in the middle of the desert!" she exclaimed. "I was expecting—I don't know—a little stream or something."

"There are not many lakes here," said Rosa, smiling. "But the lakes that we do have are very important to the wildlife and the people. There must be an underground spring here."

They walked down to the shore. The water was beautiful and clear and warm to the touch. Leah wanted to bathe in it.

"No!" Connor said suddenly. "That can't be . . . It is! It's an Amazon molly!"

Leah followed his pointing finger. There in the shallows beside a clump of reeds, she saw a small silver fish, about the length of her palm.

"This is the perfect spot for these kinds of fish," said Connor in excitement. "I can't believe I'm seeing one."

"What's so special about this fish?" Leah wanted to know.

"All Amazon mollies are female. They reproduce without males." Connor grinned at the look of surprise on

Leah's face. "They're named after the Amazon tribe of women warriors, from Greek mythology. They're so cool!"

It was pretty cool, Leah had to admit. She crouched down to get a better look at the molly. Then she leaped up with a shout.

"Wolf prints!" she said. "They're leading away from the lake! Connor was right. Our wolf must have come here for a drink!"

The prints were distinct in the damp sand that surrounded this part of the lake: the large central pad had four smaller pads around it, with the sharp indentations of claws at the tips.

Rosa shaded her eyes. "They are heading in the direction of the mountains," she said.

"Let's go get the Beagle and start driving again," Connor suggested.

They hurried back up the rocky track, past the outcrop of boulders and the large cacti. The Beagle was waiting patiently for them. Leah was looking forward to sitting underneath its shady canvas roof once more.

The Beagle gave off a blast of sharp, high-pitched beeps as they got closer. Leah stopped and looked uncertainly at Connor. "I've never heard the Beagle make that noise before," she said. "It sounds like it's warning us about something."

They moved more slowly toward the vehicle. The Beagle was flashing its lights now as well. It was definitely trying to tell them—

"Whoa!" gasped Leah.

Sitting on the Beagle's steering wheel was a large orange and black creature with a long tail. Its scales glittered in the light.

Leah felt a chill of nerves run through her at the sight of its long flickering tongue.

"Cool lizard," said Connor admiringly. He moved a little closer.

But Rosa looked alarmed. "Don't go any nearer!" she said, grasping Connor's elbow. "It's a Gila monster. Extremely venomous."

Leah had heard of these creatures. They could give a really nasty bite.

The Gila monster flicked its tongue again.

"We have to move it," Connor pointed out, "or we won't be able to drive after the wolf."

"I don't know how we can do that without hurting it, or getting bitten," Rosa admitted.

The Gila monster looked very comfortable on the Beagle's steering wheel.

Leah had a feeling it might not move for a while—not until it was hungry.

That gave her an idea.

Leah walked around to the back of the Beagle and opened the trunk. Here, she found their cooler of food and water and she began to dig through the supplies. Did Gila monsters like cheese sandwiches? There was only one way to find out.

She unwrapped the sandwich and placed it on the ground near the Beagle. Then she beckoned to the others. They all crouched quietly behind some cacti and waited.

"Why is it called a Gila monster?" Connor asked faintly as they waited for the lizard to move.

"The Gila is a river," said Rosa. "Many of them used to live there. It's not really fair that it's called a monster, even if it is venomous. Really, it is just a lizard."

The Gila monster flicked its tongue. Perhaps it was smelling the sandwich, Leah thought. Very slowly—she couldn't believe how slowly—it uncurled itself from the steering wheel and began to move. The great lizard moved at a snail's pace, placing one clawed foot carefully after the other.

"Take your time," said Connor, rolling his eyes.

Rosa laughed. "They are very slow. But quick when they are hunting their prey!"

After what felt like hours, the Gila monster reached the ground. It flicked its tongue again, and turned its head very slowly toward the sandwich. Finally, it strolled up to the sandwich and began eating.

"At last!" exclaimed Leah. "Now we can go after the trail of prints."

"It's a shame about the sandwich," said Connor, a little gloomily.

Chapter Five
PURSUIT OF THE PRINTS

The Beagle seemed as relieved as Leah, Connor and Rosa to be moving away from the Gila monster. It beeped merrily as Leah drove along.

After a few minutes, they reached the lake again, bumping and shuddering over the rocky ground. Coyotes startled and hurried away from the shore at the sound of the engine, and birds cawed and wheeled away overhead.

"The prints began here," said Leah, pointing to the damp sand with its clear impression of the wolf's paws. "And headed that way." She pointed toward the mountains.

"So what are we waiting for?" asked Connor. "Let's follow those prints!"

BEEP BEEP BEEP! said the Beagle.

Rosa laughed. "I like your buggy!"

BEEP! the Beagle said again.

"It likes you too," said Leah with a grin.

The ground soon began to rise upward. Leah carefully drove around the cacti that stood in her path, weaving an unsteady line toward the mountains. The prints were still visible in the dust. But they were getting harder to follow the farther from the lake they went.

The ground grew steeper. Leah willed the Beagle onward, but progress was slow. As they reached a particularly steep and rocky slope, the Beagle gave a long, low beep of complaint.

"You're right," Leah sighed, patting the steering wheel. "It is getting much too steep for you to carry all three of us."

"Maybe we should walk from here," suggested Rosa.

"Can we eat something first?" Connor asked hopefully.

They climbed out of the buggy. Leah headed to the trunk and pulled out some more sandwiches and bottles of water. They ate and drank gratefully, leaning against the dusty side of the Beagle.

"Perfect," Connor sighed. He rubbed his tummy in satisfaction.

Leah looked around for the wolf prints. She worried for a moment that they had lost them. But then, she spotted the faint marks beside an outcrop of rocks. "There!" she exclaimed. She looked at a narrow path that cut through the outcrop. "I think we might need to do a bit of climbing."

Connor flexed his fingers. "After that sandwich, I could climb Mount Everest," he joked.

They began to walk. The path quickly grew narrow and steep. Leah started using the rocks as handholds to pull her onward. Every so often, she could see a plant that had been flattened, with broken leaves and scattered petals.

"We're on the right track," she called back to the others, who were climbing a little way behind her. "See how the plants have been disturbed?"

"I can't see the prints any more," Connor panted.

Leah glimpsed one single, clear print in a stretch of dust and sand directly in front of her. Oddly, the print didn't show any claw marks on the tips of the pads, unlike the print beside the lake. Perhaps the wolf had worn down her claws in the climb.

As she climbed and scanned the ground for more prints, Leah almost bumped straight into a big rock. The path had ended abruptly at the foot of a short cliff.

Connor joined her. He rested his hands on his knees to catch his breath. "Great," he said, frowning. "Now what?"

Leah wasn't sure what made her look up. But as she shaded her eyes and looked toward the sky, she realized something very important.

The prints they had been following didn't belong to a wolf.

They belonged to a mountain lion, sitting on a rocky ledge directly above them.

And the mountain lion was looking straight at them.

Briefly, Leah forgot how dangerous a mountain lion could be. All she could see right now was how beautiful the animal was, with her sleek pale coat, her large paws and her beautifully shaped head.

"Lion," Connor croaked. "It's a LION!"

"A puma, actually," Leah corrected.

"Now is not the time for details!" Connor hissed.

Leah gasped aloud at the sight of two more little faces peeking down at them from the ledge. Cubs! They were no more than a couple of months old, from the look of their fuzzy little ears and their dappled, camouflaged coats.

"This is wonderful!" she said. "But . . . also bad. Very bad. Pumas can be vicious— but when they have cubs to protect as well, they can be deadly."

"I really wish you hadn't told me that," groaned Connor.

Staring at them with fierce yellow eyes, the puma gave a low, rumbling growl.

"We have to get out of here," Rosa said. Her eyes were wide and frightened.

The puma stood up and growled again. Beside her, the cubs watched them curiously.

"I think she's going to jump," said Leah. She started backing away as fast as she could, slipping a little on the steep path. "Get back, Connor!"

"But it's so high," Connor started, "she'll never make a jump like—"

The puma sprang.

It looked like she was flying. Leah wouldn't have been surprised if a pair of wings had unfurled from her pale, sandy back. She landed with a heavy thump, lashing her tail and growling. Now she was only a few yards away. Up on the rocky ledge, her cubs mewed and watched.

Connor hurriedly backed down the path and joined Leah and Rosa.

"Now what?" said Leah with a gulp as the puma glared at them, still growling.

"A friend at the conservation center once told me how to scare off a puma," said Rosa quietly. "We need to make ourselves as big as possible and then make a lot of noise."

"I don't feel very big right now," said Connor in a trembling voice.

"I will climb on you," said Rosa. "Hold still now . . ."

She scrambled up the rocks that lined the path and clambered on to Connor's shoulders. Their combined height was definitely more impressive, Leah thought.

The puma growled again. Its haunches tensed. Leah recognized the movement from her cat at home. Any minute now, it was going to pounce!

"Whoa . . ." Connor gasped, trying to stay steady as Rosa began waving her arms and shouting.

"Rarrgh!" Rosa shouted. "Come on, you have to shout too!"

"RAAARRRGH!" yelled Connor, more in terror than anything.

"You too, Leah!" called Rosa. "Make a big noise!"

The puma flattened her ears to her head and crouched lower on the path. Her tail lashed harder. Her lips curled to show long, mean yellow teeth. They were running out of time!

Leah seized a couple of large rocks and banged them together. The sound echoed harshly off the rockface.

"RAAAAAARGGGH!" she yelled, banging the rocks as hard as she could. "RAAARRRGH!!!"

The puma hissed and growled once more, before she suddenly turned and sprang away, back up the rockface toward her cubs.

Leah's legs felt weak. She dropped to the ground in relief.

They were safe!

Chapter Six
DESPERATE DEHYDRATION

Connor wiped his forehead and squinted at the wide, dusty horizon. "We're never going to find the wolf, are we?" he said miserably.

They had dropped Rosa back at the conservation center, then returned to the desert. The sun was at its highest point now, and the temperature was punishing.

And they were still no closer to finding the pregnant wolf.

Leah was feeling pretty low herself as they drove along. The Chihuahuan Desert was huge, and full of places where a pregnant wolf could hide and give birth to her cubs. They were miles from the conservation center. Miles from anywhere, really. How were they ever going to track the wolf down?

But, straightening her shoulders and

taking a deep breath, Leah turned to Connor and said, "we have to keep going. The conservation center needs us. These wolves are important. If their numbers keep dropping like Rosa says, they will soon be extinct."

Connor shuddered. "Extinct is a horrible word," he said. "Dead, gone, never to return."

"I know," Leah agreed. "So we keep looking. Right?"

"Right," said Connor. He looked hopefully at Leah. "But can we stop and eat something first?"

Leah parked the Beagle in the shade of a tall cactus. Then she and Connor climbed out and headed to the trunk.

"Whoa," said Connor.

Leah's stomach plummeted. They stared

at the single sandwich and lonely bottle of water which was all that remained of their food supplies.

"Did we really eat everything already?" asked Connor.

Leah glanced at him. "You ate everything already," she said, a little angrily. "This isn't good. What if we run out of food? More importantly, what if we run out of water?"

They stared at each other a little anxiously. The desert stretched around them like a great dusty bowl of nothing. This was an extremely serious situation.

"We need help," said Leah at last.

"The Exploration Station!" they both said together.

They hurried back to the Beagle's dashboard. Leah felt very relieved when the screen winked into life and she saw all their friends smiling at them.

"Hey!" said Gustavo. "How's the mission going?"

"Not very well," Leah confessed.

"And I ate all of our food," said Connor apologetically.

"The water is more important," said Leah. "We only have one bottle left. We need your advice. What should we do?"

"The screen is telling us you're in the Chihuahuan Desert," said Kiki. "Right?"

Leah nodded.

"We'll do some research," said Ollie. "Give us a second—we'll see what we can find."

It was an anxious wait for Leah and Connor in the shade of the cactus as their friends researched the problem.

"Got it," said Ollie at last. "You can collect water from agave plants, and you can eat prickly pears. Can you see those plants anywhere?"

Leah shaded her eyes and squinted at the ground. "I don't know," she groaned. "I can't think. I'm too hot, and too thirsty!"

Roshni appeared on the screen. "Come on, Leah," she said gently. "Plants are your thing, remember?"

"Roshni's right," Cheng said. "If that was me right now, all I could see would be the rocks!"

The others laughed.

"I'm sending you pictures of agave plants and prickly pears now," said Ollie. "Have you got them?"

Two images appeared on the screen. Leah recognized the agave with its spiky, fleshy leaves and the prickly pear with its small yellow flowers and knobbly green fruit. She had seen those plants nearby. She felt a little surge of confidence.

"Thanks guys!" Leah exclaimed. "Come on Connor—I saw those plants a little way back down this track."

"Good luck!" called the Explorers as the Beagle's screen winked off. "You can do this!"

Leah hurried down the track, following the Beagle's tire markings to make sure that they didn't deviate from the path. After a few minutes, the sharp outline of a huge agave plant loomed up on the roadside.

"It looks like a cartoon explosion," said Connor. "Do you know what I mean?"

Leah laughed as she took out her pocket knife. "Totally!" she agreed. "We'll cut off some of these leaves and take them back to the Beagle with us."

Leah and Connor carefully harvested some of the younger, juicier leaves and carried them back to their desert buggy.

They then returned to find the prickly pear plant. It was rounder and lower to the ground than the agave, with pretty, papery flowers and fat yellow droplets of fruit growing around the edges of the leaves. Leah cut off as many as they could carry between them, being careful not to spike herself on the spines. She took some of the prickly pear flowers too, and tucked them into her pocket for safekeeping.

Connor suddenly raised his head. "Can you hear that?" he said.

Floating toward them on the breeze, Leah heard the distant sound of howling.

"A wolf!" she exclaimed.

"Maybe OUR wolf," said Connor in excitement.

Leah tried to figure out which direction the howling was coming from. She tilted her head, listening carefully. "There it is again," she said, as another piercing howl swept toward them across the desert. "It's close. But where?"

The wind was picking up. Leah could feel bits of grit gathering in the air, tingling against her cheeks. "I think we're in for another dust storm," she said, looking at Connor. "We need to find shelter before we can look for the wolf. The Beagle only has a canvas roof, not canvas sides. We won't have any protection."

"I'll drive," Connor offered.

Leah quickly buckled herself in beside him, pulling her hat down over her eyes and the neck of her T-shirt up around her mouth. She hadn't enjoyed the dust storm which had greeted them on their arrival in the desert. And judging from the way the dust was swirling around the buggy, they didn't have much time to get clear of this one.

"Drive," she said. "Drive, Connor. Quickly!"

Chapter Seven
A CHANGE IN DIRECTION

The Beagle sped through the rising dust. Connor had to swerve once or twice to avoid a cactus that loomed unexpectedly in the swirling sand. Leah clung on tight. The gritty wind stung her eyes and blasted her skin. She felt it creeping under her hat, up her sleeves and around her ankles.

The dust briefly cleared and revealed looming hills. Connor put his foot down. The road was rising now, away from the flat plains, and into the rocky dips and valleys.

Leah lowered her T-shirt just enough to speak. "Look for a cave," she said. Her voice was hoarse with the dust.

"There!" Connor shouted.

Tucked into a fold in the rocky hillside, Leah saw the wide black space. Connor pulled up with a squeal of brakes, and they both jumped out of the Beagle and hurled themselves toward the cave.

The sudden change from wind and dust to cool darkness was an intense relief. Leah wearily tugged her T-shirt away from her face. Closing her eyes, she enjoyed her first lungful of clean cave air.

Connor had taken off his hat and was shaking his head. Sand scattered on to his shoulders. "I've got sand everywhere," he complained. "And I mean everywhere."

Leah sank down to rest on the rocky cave floor. Connor sank down beside her.

"Now what do we do?" he said.

"I guess we wait out the storm," she replied.

The wind swirled in great yellow clouds outside. Leah and Connor watched it from the safety of the cave.

"I'm hungry," Connor said after a while.

"When are you not?" Leah teased. "Come on. We'll wait for a dip in the wind and go get our supplies from the Beagle."

There was a camping stove in the trunk of the Beagle, as well as the last remaining sandwich and bottle of water. There were also the prickly pears they'd collected, and the agave leaves. After sharing the sandwich, Leah set a camping pot on top of the flame to boil. Then she added the prickly pears. Slicing up the agave leaves into thick chunks, she stripped off the tough outer skin and handed the slimy innards to Connor.

"Not exactly a cola, is it?" Connor said a little sadly.

It wasn't, that was for sure. But it was better than nothing. So were the prickly pears, which reminded Leah a little of watermelon due to their juicy pink insides. Cooking them had softened their sharp little spines, and made them easier to peel.

"I hope the wolf managed to find shelter, too," said Connor, munching on a prickly pear. "It can't be much fun for the animals out there right now."

"Animals know how to take care of themselves," Leah said. "I'm sure she'll be fine."

The dust storm was clearing. Leah and Connor packed away their stove and headed back outside. Now that the visibility had improved, Leah could see that they were in a valley, with a network of caves spread around the hillside.

The Beagle was in a sorry state. It had dust and sand all over its seats and dashboard. It beeped a little sadly as Leah tried to clean it up. But that wasn't the worst of their problems. The sand had covered up their tracks completely. There was no hope of finding any wolf prints now. All they had left to go on was the howling they'd heard earlier.

Leah sighed, wondering when their mission was going to get easier.

"What's that?" asked Connor suddenly.

A dark cloud of smoke was swirling out of one of the caves further up the hillside.

"Is it another dust storm?" Connor suggested anxiously.

The smoke was breaking up into smaller black chunks. With sudden relief, Leah made out hundreds of flapping wings and furry little bodies. "It's not dust," she exclaimed. "It's a flock of bats!"

The cloud of bats swooped over their heads. Leah glimpsed long, flexible black snouts and bright eyes amid the soft, leathery mass of wings. "They're probably Mexican free-tailed bats," she guessed.

"Looks like there's plenty of them here," Connor observed.

Leah frowned. "I guess. Although it's weird, the way they're flying in the daytime. They usually come out at night. Something must have disturbed them."

She looked back at the cave the bats had emerged from. It was smaller than the rest, and looked as if it was set quite deep into the hillside.

Leah made a decision. "Come on," she said to Connor. "Let's check it out."

"To the bat cave!" Connor cried. He laughed. "I've always wanted to say that."

They made their way down the valley.
Leah kept her eyes firmly fixed on the cave as
they walked toward it. She was afraid she
might forget which one it was otherwise.
After a short scramble up a rocky slope and
a little bit of climbing, they reached the
black cave mouth.

Connor wrinkled his nose. "Weird smell,"
he said. "Kind of makes me . . . hungry?"

"That'll be the bats," said Leah, laughing at the look on Connor's face. "People say they smell like tortilla chips."

"I get that!" Connor exclaimed. His tummy rumbled. "My stomach gets that too," he added.

They moved cautiously into the dim interior. The cave seemed to go back some distance, and was cozy and dark.

Then Leah heard it. A gentle, snuffling sound. She put her fingers to her lips and motioned to Connor.

Through the gloom, they saw a shape snuggled deep into the cave. Actually, they saw several shapes—moving, mewling shapes.

They had found the missing wolf—and her newborn cubs!

Chapter Eight
FAREWELL TO NEW FRIENDS

Leah and Connor sat together on the ledge outside the cave, swinging their legs in the Mexican sun. The conservation experts had arrived a few minutes earlier, after Leah had called them on the Beagle's radio, and the cave was a bustle of cautious activity. No one wanted to disturb or worry the mother wolf at such a delicate time, but it was important for the breeding program to monitor the cubs and make sure they grew up to be healthy and strong. Therefore, the technicians were setting up a neat little webcam just inside the cave mouth, with the lens trained on the new wolf family.

Rosa had come too, and was helping with the generator and the wiring for the cameras.

"Come and look," she said, smiling and motioning Leah and Connor over to the monitor outside the cave.

Leah and Connor joined Rosa to gaze at the monitor. It was dim, but they could make out the mother wolf happily licking her cubs. The cubs only looked like they were a few days old, with fuzzy coats and ears that hadn't unfolded yet. They were wriggling and feeding hungrily. Every now and then,

the mother wolf's eyes flashed green in the night-vision light of the monitor. It seemed as if the conservationists were being watched, too.

"Thank you for finding them," said one of the experts, a smiling man with a heavy beard, who Rosa had introduced as Raoul. "I can't describe to you how important they are. There are so few of these wolves left in the wild, so every cub matters."

"And now you've got four," said Leah with a grin.

Raoul laughed. "Yes, we do!"

"Why did she come to this cave to have her cubs instead of having them in her den at the center?" Connor wanted to know.

Raoul scratched his head. "We aren't sure," he admitted.

"Perhaps because the cave is bigger and darker than the den at the center," Leah suggested.

"That is a very good point," said Raoul. "We will look at building a den to match this cave, and see if the wolves like it."

"This wolf does, anyway," said Connor with a smile.

The technicians finished with the generator and joined Leah, Connor, Raoul and Rosa, smiling and celebrating. It had been a good day.

"Thank you for all your help," said Rosa, hugging Leah and Connor tightly. "This is a wonderful start for our program. The Mexican wolves have a lot to thank you both for."

"It's been a privilege," said Leah honestly.

She and Connor took one last look at the wolf and her cubs, who looked snuggly and safe in their cave haven. Then, with one last wave to Rosa and the other conservationists, they headed back to the valley floor, where the Beagle waited patiently.

Connor gave Leah a high five as they climbed into the desert buggy. "Mission accomplished," he said with satisfaction.

Leah started the Beagle's engine. With a loud, low roar, the buggy accelerated away into a flash of dazzling white light. The hot sandy wind of the Mexican desert swirled around them as Leah felt the steering wheel of the Beagle twist and change. The comfy padded seat beneath her became hard, dented metal once again, and the loose desert clothing transformed back into their familiar jeans and T-shirts.

And then . . . they were back where they had started: sitting in a broken-down go-kart in the middle of the gleaming black floor of the Exploration Station.

"You made it!" exclaimed Ollie, as Leah and Connor unbuckled themselves. "After that call you made, we were worried."

"Your advice was great," said Connor cheerfully. "We were able to get both food and water from those plants. Although I might give agave leaves a pass next time. They were pretty slimy!"

"So you found the wolf?" asked Cheng.

Leah told the others all about the conservation center, and the lake, and the caves, and of course the mother wolf and her four perfect cubs. Then she dug inside her jeans pocket and pulled out the bright

flowers of the prickly pear plant.

"Pretty, aren't they?" she said, twirling them between her fingers. "Who'd have thought you could pick flowers in the desert?"

She opened up one of the display cases, tucked the flowers into a little vase and gently shut the glass door. The flowers looked colorful and fresh against the muted fossils and stones that the Secret Explorers

had collected on their adventures.

Glowing doors began to appear among the walls of the Exploration Station. It was time to go home.

"See you, Connor," said Leah, giving her mission mate a hug.

"Until next time!" said Connor with a grin.

With a wave to the others, Leah stepped through the nearest door. She closed her eyes in the dazzling light, enjoying the cool sensation of the wind that blew through her hair.

Stepping out into the brightness of her garden, Leah shaded her eyes and breathed in the gorgeous, growing smell around her.

"There you are, Leah!" said her mom, walking through the backyard toward her.

Leah noticed that her mother was hiding something behind her back. "What have you got there?" she asked curiously.

Her mother produced a little pot. "A plant for you," she said proudly. "They were selling them at the market this morning. I thought you'd like it!"

Leah stared in delight. It was a bright green succulent, with plump leaves that she knew stored water. It was in the same family of plants as the cacti she'd seen on the mission. "Thanks, Mom!" she exclaimed.

Looking around, she saw the perfect spot to plant it: a sunny little corner of the flower bed, near her calendulas. She smiled as her fingers pressed down the soft earth around the little plant. It would always remind her of her mission in the Chihuahuan Desert!

MISSION NOTES

The Chihuahuan Desert is the largest desert in North America, stretching all the way from the southwestern United States and into the center of the Mexican Highlands. It is more than 200,000 sq miles (518,000 sq km).

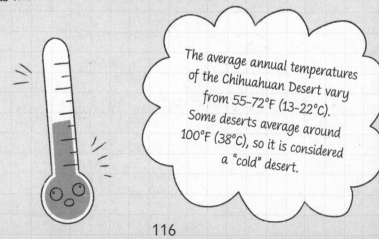

The average annual temperatures of the Chihuahuan Desert vary from 55-72°F (13-22°C). Some deserts average around 100°F (38°C), so it is considered a "cold" desert.

PLENTIFUL PLANTS

More than 3,500 plant species thrive in the Chihuahuan Desert. This includes more cacti species than any other desert, and one-fifth of the world's estimated 1,500 cacti species.

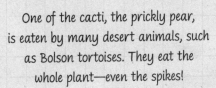

One of the cacti, the prickly pear, is eaten by many desert animals, such as Bolson tortoises. They eat the whole plant—even the spikes!

The Soaptree Yucca plant is one of the most common plants found in the Chihuahuan Desert. As its name suggests, this fascinating perennial plant (one that lasts a long time) can produce a natural soap.

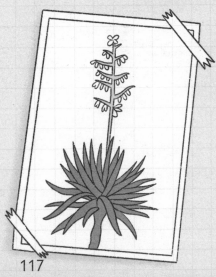

MEXICAN WOLVES

FACT FILE

* **Latin name**: *Canis lupus baileyi*
* **Animal type**: Mammal—The Mexican wolf is a subspecies of the gray wolf. They are often referred to as "el lobo," which means 'the wolf' in Spanish
* **Location**: North America—In southeastern Arizona and southern New Mexico in the United States, and in northern Mexico
* **Length**: Approx 53 in (135 cm)
* **Weight**: 60-100 lbs (27-45 kg) (about the same as a large dog)

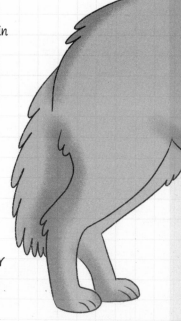

IN ANCIENT TIMES, MEXICAN WOLVES WERE WORSHIPPED BY PEOPLE, SINCE THEY WERE CONSIDERED TO BE ONE OF THE SYMBOLS OF THE GOD OF THE SUN.

There used to be thousands of Mexican wolves, but from 1915, the US started controlling the population to stop them from preying on farm animals. By the 1970s, Mexican wolves were almost wiped out, with only a few remaining in captivity.

CONSERVATION EFFORTS

In 1998, a conservation program released 11 Mexican wolves back into the wild, and their numbers have slowly grown ever since. They remain the most endangered subspecies of wolf in the world, so efforts continue to be made to protect them and restore their numbers.

ANIMALS OF THE CHIHUAHUAN DESERT

JAVELINA

One of the many interesting animals that can be found in the Chihuahuan Desert are javelina (also known as collared peccary). These piglike animals live in packs of around 10, but some herds are as large as 50 .They are herbivores and eat native plants such as agave.

COYOTE

One of javelina's main predators is the coyote. Coyotes make "singing" noises to communicate with other coyotes and keep track of their own pack. They are not picky eaters and are classed as omnivores, which means they eat plants and meat.

MOUNTAIN LION

Another of javelina's main predators is the mountain lion. They are called "the cat of many names," and these include mountain lion, cougar, panther, puma, painter, el leon, and catamount.

The Chihuahuan Desert is home to more than 500 species of bird, 130 species of mammal, 100 species of fish, and 170 species of amphibians and reptiles, including the following:

Mule deer

Pronghorn

Kit fox

Prairie dog

Roadrunner

Earless lizard

Golden eagle

Black-tailed jackrabbit

QUIZ

1   What can Texas horned lizards shoot from the side of their eyes to scare off predators?

2   True or false: Over ninety percent of the world's rattlesnakes live in Mexico.

3   What do desert tarantulas do to shelter them from the heat?

4   True or false: All Amazon mollies are female.

5   What are Gila monsters named after?

6   True or false: Pumas can't jump very high.

7   What food do people say that bats smell like?

Check your answers on page 127

GLOSSARY

BEACHCOMBING

Searching a beach area, looking for items of value, interest, or use.

CHASSIS

The structural frame of a vehicle, usually including the wheels and engine.

DAPPLED

Marked with spots or patches.

DEHYDRATION

A condition caused by the loss of fluid. When the body doesn't have as much water as it needs, it can be dangerous.

DEVIATE

To move in a different direction from your planned path.

EVAPORATION

A liquid turning into a gas.

GENERATOR
A machine that converts one kind of energy into another in order to power objects, such as a webcam.

HOARSE
A rough or weak-sounding voice.

INDENTATIONS
Holes or marks in the surface of something, such as the ground.

LOOMED
An object which has come into sight as a large, unclear shape, often in the distance.

MEWLING
Soft, high-pitched crying sound.

OUTCROP
A large rock, or group of rocks, that sticks out from the ground.

REFUGE
A place that offers shelter or protection.

ROCKFACE
The steep, vertical side of a rock.

SUCCULENT
A plant, such as a cactus, with thick leaves and a stem that can hold a lot of water. These are often found in dry, desertlike areas.

UNFURLED
When something that was previously rolled up gets unfolded and expands.

VENOMOUS
A venomous animal can release venom through a sting or fangs. This substance may be deadly if injected into an animal or plant.

Quiz answers

1. Blood

2. True

3. Dig burrows

4. True

5. The Gila River

6. False—they can jump as high as 18ft (5m) and as far as 45ft (14m)

7. Tortilla chips

DK | Penguin Random House

FSC MIX Paper from responsible sources FSC™ C018179 www.fsc.org

For Myia and Bodhi

Text for DK by Working Partners Ltd
9 Kingsway, London WC2B 6XF
With special thanks to Lucy Courtenay

Design by Collaborate Ltd
Illustrator Ellie O'Shea
Consultant Anita Ganeri

Acquisitions Editor James Mitchem
Editor Becca Arlington
US Senior Editor Shannon Beatty
Designer Sonny Flynn
Publishing Coordinator Issy Walsh
Senior Production Editor Nikoleta Parasaki
Production Controller Ena Matagic
Publishing Director Sarah Larter

First American Edition, 2023
Published in the United States by DK Publishing
1745 Broadway, 20th Floor, New York, New York 10019

Printed and bound in Great Britain by
Clays Ltd, Elcograf S.p.A.

www.dk.com
For the curious